Come Bake with Ellen Grape

ANGIE ELLISON

To order additional copies of this book, contact:
Xlibris
844-714-8691
www.Xlibris.com
Orders@Xlibris.com

ISBN: Softcover   978-1-6698-6843-9
        Hardcover   978-1-6698-6844-6
        EBook   978-1-6698-6842-2

Print information available on the last page

Rev. date: 02/22/2023

ELLEN GRAPE'S CHOCOLATE CUPCAKES

1 Box super moist chocolate cake mix
1 ¼ cup water
1/3 cup vegetable oil
3 eggs
1 ½ cups mini chocolate chips

Set oven to 350

Line cupcake pan with cupcake liners
I love to use pink or purple – they are my favorites

In a bowl, mix all ingredients together adding chocolate chips last. Fill cups about ¾ full. Bake until center of cupcake comes out clean when inserting a toothpick to test.

Let cupcakes cool. Frost with your favorite can frosting and your most favorite sprinkles. These are my favorite's cupcakes EVER.

Hi, my name is Ellen Grape.
Come to my class
See what I'll bake.

3

I love to bake
For family and friends
So easy and fun
Let's begin

Today, Its cupcakes
Chocolate, I think.
With fluffy white icing
And sprinkles of pink.

With my measuring cup
Pan and spoon
It won't take long
They will be ready soon.

This big
red bowl
Is for the
cake batter

10

I might
sneak a
taste
But that
won't matter.

11

In goes water, eggs
Oil and chocolate chips
The extra chocolate
Is my secret tip

The oven is set
As the recipe said
Once they have cooled
The icing I'll spread

Mom will help
Put the pan in for me
Safety, comes first.
Always you see

Excited to see
What everyone brings
All will be sold
And left not a thing.

Bake
sale

19

They are done
How pretty, they are
Now, let's keep going
We have done great so far.

My fluffy white icing
Comes in a can
I've used it before
I'll use it again

23

Yay, the icing is on
And sprinkles adorn
Just a few more candies
Or, maybe more.

This one is very special
It's just for me
Since I am the baker
Don't you agree

All pretty and boxed
Ready to show
Our class is now over
It's time to go

Ellen Grape's Chocolate Cupcakes

Here is my recipe
For you my friend
Put it away
To use it again

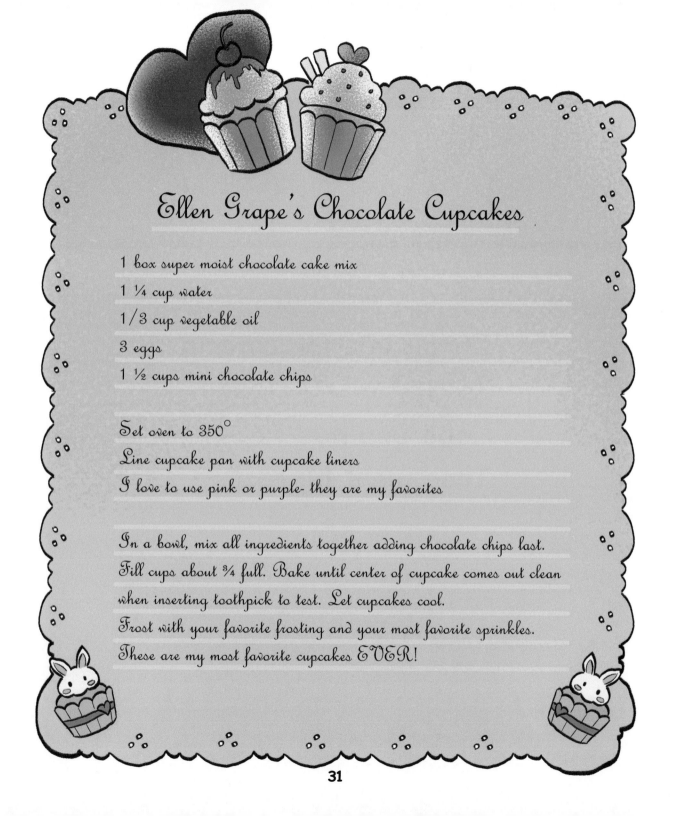

Ellen Grape's Chocolate Cupcakes

1 box super moist chocolate cake mix

1 ¼ cup water

1/3 cup vegetable oil

3 eggs

1 ½ cups mini chocolate chips

Set oven to 350°

Line cupcake pan with cupcake liners

I love to use pink or purple- they are my favorites

In a bowl, mix all ingredients together adding chocolate chips last.
Fill cups about ¾ full. Bake until center of cupcake comes out clean
when inserting toothpick to test. Let cupcakes cool.
Frost with your favorite frosting and your most favorite sprinkles.
These are my most favorite cupcakes EVER!

Thank you for coming
To my baking class
Hope you had fun
Time went by fast

Now, get in the kitchen
And make yummy treats
Because the best part of baking
Is when it's time to eat.

Your friend,

Ellen Grape

Your Friend,

Ellen Grape

Printed in the United States
by Baker & Taylor Publisher Services